To ... Lee

Tits
&
Teeth

By

Lee Richmond

A Word From the Author

I have been in love with sharks since I was a young boy. I remember watching Jaws for the first time and being terrified yet enthralled by the idea of being so completely at the mercy of something that had spent millions of years evolving into the perfect killing machine. Sharks were deadly, and should you find yourself in the presence of this aquatic terminator, that would be the story of you. Or at least that's what the movies would let you believe.

As I grew older, my interest in sharks, and especially the Great White, also grew. I binged documentaries and read extensively on the subject. I discovered that pop culture had done a disservice to these beautiful, peaceful, magnificent creatures. Sharks were not the mindless killing machines that films such as Jaws and The Shallows portrayed them to be.

Digging even deeper, I learned about the shark finning trade, where sharks are caught and have their fins removed, because apparently shark fin soup is a delicacy in some countries, such as China, and then tossed back into the ocean, where they die, mutilated and unable to defend themselves.

Sharks are not mindless killing machines; people are. Human beings are cruel, heartless predators. Sharks kill to survive; humans kill for pleasure or profit.

I wrote this story as an homage to my love of shark attack horror stories. It in no way reflects the true nature of the Great White Shark. They are not vindictive or malevolent. It is purely entertainment (at least, I hope it entertains).

The shark finning industry needs to stop before sharks become just another animal that human beings hunt to extinction.

For more information about the protection of sharks, or to make a donation, please visit The Shark Trust at https://www.sharktrust.org/

For:
My ever-supportive wife whose love and patience knows no bounds. My mum, who is also supportive and reads everything I write, even though she isn't a fan of horror. And, finally, my good friend Mark, who patiently proofreads this nonsense and doesn't mock my many hilarious spelling mistakes, grammatical errors and continuity cockups.

Against:
The shark finning trade and the fishing industry. Fuck you all.

Appetiser

It was a rare thing for Madison Lock to admit she was wrong. When her husband, Daniel, had first suggested they holiday on Bonato Beach, otherwise known as The Mecca of Skin, she'd assumed he'd suffered a stroke or minor head trauma.

Her initial reaction had been to laugh it off. No way was she going to spend her precious vacation time at some 'nudist beach.' Besides, based on what she knew about the reality of those places, they were generally a sausage fest. Scores of horny guys who turn up expecting to see some titties, only to arrive and find a bunch of other guys with the same hopes and dreams, thereby having said hopes brutally dashed by the lack of female flesh on display. Just a gathering of dudes stood around with their sad, disappointed peckers shrivelling in the sun, trying not to make eye contact with each other or each other's peckers.

Daniel's persistence soon clarified that he was indeed serious. He'd read about it in Playboy of all places and had concluded that not only would it be incredibly liberating, but it might also add a little spark back to their marriage. Something that, she had to admit, had been lacking of late.

Of course she'd argued. She'd made it clear that she only had a limited number of vacation days each year, and she wasn't interested in using them so that her husband could sunbathe while eyeing up naked women. He'd sworn that this wasn't what the holiday would be about. How it would do them both the world of good and how it might help sweep away some of the tedium that had peppered their lives of late.

Eventually, as she always did, Madison had given in. *'Anything for a quiet life,'* she'd thought. And with that, they'd packed and flown off to the largest naturist destination in the South Pacific.

The warm, crystal-clear water felt amazing against her naked body. It was amusing for her to think that just a week ago, she wouldn't even shower in front of her husband. Sure, he saw her naked on the odd occasion that they had sex, but, other than that, Madison was far too self-conscious to parade around the house minus her clothes. Yet here she was, four days into a two-week holiday, and she hadn't worn a stitch since the day they'd arrived. Daniel had been right. It was liberating.

It was hotel policy that once a guest arrived, their clothing would be surrendered to the staff at the Olive Refuge Resort to be stored in a lockbox. Clothing could only be retrieved once a guest reached the end of their stay, or on the odd occasion that they wished to leave the resort and explore other parts of the island. In its twenty-five years of operation, no guest had ever felt the need to wander further. The Mecca of Skin had everything anyone would ever need, and its visitors were far too busy having fun to warrant excursions elsewhere.

Madison lay floating on her back, the warm rays of the sun washing over her saltwater-soaked skin, and she struggled to remember a time when she'd felt so relaxed. Everything seemed perfect. They hadn't gotten on this well in years, but since their arrival at the resort, they'd felt like a couple of love-struck teenagers again. Not only had Madison been wrong, but she couldn't have been happier about it.

A faint voice penetrated her daydream. Loud enough that she was aware of it, but not so loud that she could hear what it said. She looked over to the shore, taking a moment to register how far she'd drifted from the beach, and saw Daniel waving frantically. He continued to shout, but she couldn't make out what he was yelling about.

"Hey, honey," she called back with a smile and a wave.

He continued hollering and waving his arms about.

'Maybe, it's lunchtime,' she thought, suddenly aware of how hungry she felt. Breakfast seemed so long ago, and she figured it wouldn't hurt to make her way back and grab a bite to eat.

"Coming back now," she called back to where Daniel stood, throwing his arms over his head like a maniac.

"Calm down," she grumbled, beginning her swim back to dry land.

Madison had covered about ten feet before the first attack. The pain wasn't instant, just the sensation of something pulling on her leg, gently at first.

"What the fuck?" she muttered, confused.

The second tug was much harder, dragging her underwater, and that's when the pain kicked in. A sudden, sharp, excruciating sting travelled up her left leg. In her panic, she'd taken a breath just as her head had submerged beneath the surf, and her lungs throbbed with the unexpected introduction of saltwater. The surrounding water turned from crystal blue to bright red as Madison thrashed to break free from the grip of whatever had ahold of her.

A second wave of agony shot through her system, followed by another sharp, excruciating tug, and then

Madison was free. Gathering her senses, she made a break for it, pulling herself up with all the strength she could muster until she breached the surface, expelling the seawater from her aching lungs with a splutter.

After taking a moment to fill her lungs with fresh air, Madison realised the seriousness of the situation she now found herself in. She bobbed gently on the waves, surrounded by what she knew to be her blood.

Her hand worked its way down her thigh to investigate the injury that screamed its way up her nervous system and into her brain. Her heart pounded against her rib cage with the discovery that she ceased to be below the knee. Whatever had attacked her had taken the rest of her leg with it.

Her eyes scanned the beach, frantically searching for Daniel, who no longer stood waving. When she finally spotted him he was in the water, his arms pounding through the waves like the wheel of a steamboat as he tried desperately to reach her. She had drifted so far from the shore that he might as well have been on the other side of the island.

"Help me!" she screamed, thrashing her arms in the water to draw attention to herself. "Somebody, fucking help me!"

More naked bodies lined the shore now as onlookers gathered to see what all the commotion was about. A couple of them ran into the sea to join Daniel on his rescue mission. Even in her shocked, anguished state, Madison could find humour in what she was witnessing. To her, it looked like a pornographic episode of Baywatch. *'Even more pornographic episode of Baywatch,'* she thought.

Had she been less distracted by her thoughts on whether Baywatch classed as soft porn, she might have been aware of the large, dark shape that charged up behind her. She may also have spotted the sleek dorsal fin that broke the surface moments before impact. As it was, Madison Lock remained blissfully unaware of what was coming for her. The last thing she would see before having her ticket punched would be the collection of male genitals of all shapes and sizes and a variety of breasts from the small and pert to the basketball-sized and ridiculous. Dairy Bombs, as Daniel liked to call them.

Daniel Lock knew he wouldn't reach his wife in time. He saw the fin, saw the beast as it breached the surface, and saw it hit Madison like a diesel train.

The Shark took Madison into its mouth headfirst. Its nightmarish maw of razor-sharp teeth came crashing down on her skull with such force that her cranium split like a melon before she could so much as scream. Blood and brain matter squirted into the water like a squeezed tomato as the fish chewed on the woman's head until its saw-like jaws decapitated her just above the top lip, leaving the lower half of her face and neck still attached.

Madison's body floated limply in her own gruesome mess as the sea beast circled back.

Daniel watched helplessly as the shark took his wife's body into the depths.

Soup

Around the same time as Madison Lock's unfortunate encounter with the Great White, patrons of the Olive Refuge Resort busied themselves boarding the resort's private yacht for the Naked Neptune Tour.

Less of a tour of anything in particular and more of a good excuse to head out to sea and party in your birthday suit, the Naked Neptune Tour was always a popular activity amongst the island's guests, whether they be first-timers or seasoned veterans.

The brochure promised sun, sea, dancing and as many free cocktails as you could tip down your neck before putting yourself into a coma. And all at the very reasonable price of twenty-five dollars.

DJ Jammin, or MC Thor's Hammer as the guests called him based on the ludicrous size of his penis, stood at the top of the gangplank greeting revellers as they came aboard for their day of sea-bound hedonism.

Two naked, surgically augmented blondes draped themselves over each of Jammin's arms.

"Step aboard, you beautifully unclad, unveiled landlubbers. We have such sights to show you. Get ready to let it all hang out aboard our luxury yacht as we set sail for the sexy, open sea."

"I should never have let you talk me into this, Chris," Ollie Beeker complained as he hurried up the ramp to prevent the weird, fat guy with the bushy white beard from brushing up against his rear end, as he had been trying to do the entire time they had been queuing. Every time he'd turned to challenge the guy, he was met with a creepy, toothless grin that suggested that pushing his tubby, naked body against much younger men was intentional.

"Don't be such a pussy, Ollie," his much larger friend called back. "This is gonna be legendary. Look at all these sexy, naked as the day they were born cum-dumpsters."

"Fucking pig," a girl with long black hair and a disgusted expression on her face barked as she pushed past him.

"You've just talked yourself off of my fuck list," Chris yelled after her.

"Eat a dick," the girl replied, giving him the finger.

"Was that entirely necessary?" Ollie asked, catching up with his friend.

"Welcome aboard, boys," DJ Jammin greeted them as they approached the top of the ramp.

"Dude," Chris replied, going in for a fist bump, which Jammin gamely responded to.

Ollie pushed his thick-rimmed glasses up his sweaty nose, only to be greeted at eye level by Jammin's enormous swaying member.

"While you're down there," Jammin said with a laugh.

"Erm, shit. Sorry," Ollie said, his face flushing red.

"Relax, kid," Jammin replied, grabbing Ollie by the hand and pulling him onto the deck. "It's just a cock."

"Oh, that's not just any cock," the girl on Jammin's left said, licking her lips.

Ollie, not knowing where to look, shuffled away as fast as he could, his cheeks the colour of beetroot.

"Jesus Christ," Jammin said, eyeing up the hefty blonde who shuffled up the ramp towards them. Her face flushed red, and sweat trickled down her face and dripped from the end of her nose. Each step appeared exhausting under her weighty frame.

"You're gonna need a bigger boat," the girl to Jammin's right sniggered.

"She's the last of them," the girl on his left informed him.

"Okay party people, gather round," Jammin called out. "As you may already be aware, my name is DJ

Jammin, and I will be your humble host on this fine day. This gorgeous gal to my right is Anita, and to my left we have the beautiful Riley. Anything you need, don't hesitate to call on them."

"I know exactly what I need from them!" Chris shouted from the crowd, much to the amusement of the other partygoers.

"Yeah, I know what you need too, son," Jammin replied. "You need a cold shower and a tall glass of shut the fuck up juice."

The group laughed again, only this time at Chris, which he didn't appreciate.

"Okay," Jammin continued. "Just a few things. We have a few safety rules and regs. Few being the operative word, so don't worry. We'll take you through those when we get out into open water."

Anita handed Jammin a clipboard.

"Thanks, honey," he said, his eyes drifting to her breasts.

Anita tapped the clipboard in his hands impatiently.

"Sorry," Jammin said, snapping out of the trance her bare chest had brought about. "I'm your party captain, but let me introduce you to the actual captain of this vessel, Captain Cunt."

Anita leaned over and whispered in his ear.

"Captain Clint," Jammin corrected. "Sorry, weird font."

Captain Clint looked on, unamused. It was the first year that they had assigned him to captain the party boat, having taken over from Captain Rockford, who'd just retired, and he'd been less than thrilled about his new post.

Captain Clint had commanded Naval Destroyers during both Gulf Wars. He'd launched countless stinger missile attacks on enemy locations and actively helped protect cargo ships from Somali pirates. How the hell he'd ended up as the captain of a party boat full of naked drunks was far beyond his comprehension.

DJ Jammin didn't notice the glare of the disapproving captain, being far too preoccupied with the collection of naked flesh that stood before him, hanging on to his every word.

"Okay, everyone. Get your beautiful behinds over to the bar and let's let our freak flags fly."

The crowd erupted in a cheer as the revellers did as instructed and headed to the poolside bar.

The ship's horn blasted, signalling its departure as the party boat headed out to sea. Everyone onboard was too busy knocking back cocktails and gyrating to the music pumping out of the ludicrously big PA speakers. Not one person noticed the huge fin that sliced through the water, following them on their journey.

Main Course

"I don't get it," Chris said, shaking his head in exasperation.

"What don't you get?" Ollie asked.

"We are thousands of miles from our homes and jobs. We're aboard a boat that has just set sail from our tropical paradise hotel. There are wall-to-wall babes, and not one of them is wearing a stitch, and you're sitting there looking like somebody pissed in your beer. What the fuck is that about?"

Chris was right. Ollie felt miserable, and he knew he shouldn't be. He wasn't a keen traveller, and he certainly wasn't the adventurous type. Chris had hounded him relentlessly to come on this vacation until Ollie had snapped and agreed to it to shut him up. He was aware that he didn't fit in. The exhibitionist life wasn't for him. His scrawny frame already caused him to feel self-conscious, and now he could add penis envy to his list of woes.

"Seriously, dude. It's titty city here. Nobody gives a shit. Nobody is looking at you and judging your pork pencil. Get your ass out of that sun-lounger and start having some fun."

"I will, Chris. Just give me a few minutes to get my head in the game, and I'll be fine. Promise."

"Oh shit, look at this," Chris said, pointing at the big girl they'd seen boarding earlier.

"Stop pointing, man. She'll see."

"That girl is a hog, bro."

Ollie shook his head in disgust. "You're being an asshole."

"Are you trying to tell me that she's not a beast? I mean, look at her ham hocks."

"Okay, I admit she's a big girl, but she has a pretty face. I bet she looks great when she's dolled up a bit."

"Ollie, my boy, you know what you get when you put lipstick on a pig?"

"No, but I have a feeling you're going to tell me."

"You get a pig in lipstick."

"Wow, you're an awful person," Ollie said in disbelief.

"Fuck this shit," Chris replied. "I'm going to get a pina colada."

Ollie watched his friends naked behind shimmy over towards the bar, and in that moment, he realised what a prick Chris was.

DJ Jammin climbed up on the stage at the end of the pool carrying a microphone and addressed the crowd.

"How're we all doing, sexy people? You all having a good time?"

The crowd whooped and cheered in response.

Maggie Madsen still hadn't gotten her head around being naked in front of strangers. Her friends had been the ones to talk her into coming out to the island, and once she'd made her mind up to tag along, she figured it wouldn't be so awkward if everyone was to be in a state of constant undress. She was wrong. Maggie still felt very uncomfortable and incredibly self-conscious. She stood with her arms folded across her chest, covering her breasts as she often did to make herself feel less exposed.

"Still feeling shy?" her friend Sarah asked.

"You know I am," Maggie replied.

"You should uncover those puppies. Do you even know how gorgeous you are? I'd kill for your figure."

Sarah was right. Maggie was an extraordinarily attractive woman. A fact that seemed lost on Maggie.

"Shut up," Maggie responded, embarrassed.

"Check out Thor's Hammer," Sarah chuckled.

"Oh, dear god," Maggie said, shielding her eyes. "He's got a boner."

DJ Jammin did indeed have an erection. His enormous member stuck out like Schwarzenegger's forearm. Not that he seemed to care as he went about entertaining the guests.

Maggie did everything in her power to not stare at it. Sarah, however, couldn't take her eyes off the thing. She tracked its movement as it swayed from side to side like she was watching a tennis match.

"Don't look directly at it," Maggie said.

"It's a penis, not the sun," Sarah replied, mocking her prudish friend. "Besides, look around you. Everyone either has a hard-on or at least a semi. It's boner town."

"That's horrible."

"It's to be expected. All this sun, sea, cocktails, and skin grinding against everyone else's skin. Boners are almost mandatory at this point."

"Well, I think it's vulgar, and if anybody so much as touches me with one of those things, I'm cutting it off."

"Maybe if you let someone touch you with one of those things from time to time, it might make you lighten up a little," Sarah said with a laugh.

"I'm okay as I am, but thanks for the prognosis, Doctor Dicklicker."

Jammin continued jumping around the stage, getting the crowd worked up as his excitable meat stick stood proudly before him. Nobody other than Maggie Madsen seemed to care.

"Go get yourselves another drink," Jammin instructed. "You have about half an hour before we start our first game, Pirate Plank Trivia. Anyone wishing to play can come and see either Anita or Riley, and they will sign you up. Don't be shy. They don't bite. Well, unless you ask nicely."

Jammin slapped both of the girls on their bare behinds. Anita, not seeming to mind one bit, beamed at the feel of his hand on her butt cheek. Riley, on the other hand, didn't share her partner's enthusiasm at being touched on the tush by this misogynistic pig. She shot him a filthy look before taking two large steps to the side to put a little distance between them.

Hordes of revellers visited the girls to put themselves forward for the first of the games, even though none of them was entirely sure what Pirate Plank Trivia was. They would soon find out.

"Okay folks, gather round for the Pirate Plank Trivia."
Everyone surged forwards, fighting one another to get to the front. This led to some opportunistic sex pests trying their luck at getting to grope some girls. They

figured that, in the chaos, nobody would know whose hands belonged to who. Strangely, no one protested.

"I'll explain the rules as we go," Jammin continued. He checked his list of names. "Do we have a Rob Kelly here?"

"Whoo, yeah," came an excitable voice as a blonde-haired surfer type with extensive tattoo work covering his arms and chest bounded from out of the crowd.

"Nice to meet you, Rob," Jammin said, extending his hand to the lad, who enthusiastically shook it in return.

"Here's how we play the game," Jammin explained. "We have a plank sticking out over the sea. There are five lines marked on the plank, and I will give you a series of trivia questions. Each time you get a question right, you stay where you are. Get one wrong, and you step towards the next line. There are ten questions overall, and your job is to still be standing on the plank by the time we get to question number ten. Keep getting them wrong, and you'll be in the sea long before then. Are you ready, Rob?"

Rob nodded emphatically.

"Great. Step up to the plank then, son."

Rob stepped up and stood at the plank. "Ready when you are," he shouted before whooping and hollering once again.

"I'm loving your enthusiasm, Rob. Okay, question one. What was Gandhi's first name?"

Rob stood for a moment as if trying to locate the answer in some dark recess of his mind. He wasn't fooling anyone, though, as it was perfectly obvious that he hadn't got a clue.

"Is it Goosey?" Rob answered with a question.

"Fucking Goosey?" Jammin said, unable to hide his bemusement at such a ridiculous reply. "What makes you think it's fucking Goosey?"

Rob looked instantly offended by the DJ's response. The spectators roared with laughter.

"You know?" Rob said. "Like the song about Goosey Gander."

This only made Jammin laugh harder. "I said Gandhi. That is the wrong answer. Take a step forward, please."

Rob did as he was asked and begrudgingly took a step towards the next line.

"Okay, question number two. In the Lord's Prayer, what word beginning with H, meaning blessed, comes before be thy name?"

Rob took another moment. He wanted to really think about his answer rather than risk making a fool of himself once again.

"I need an answer," Jammin said.

"Howard," Rob answered with a self-assured smile.

"I'm sorry, what?"

"Howard," Rob repeated. "Howard be thy name."

More laughter erupted from the crowd. Rob's cheeks flushed red with embarrassment.

"You might as well save us all some time and jump in the water now," Jammin said. "Take another step forward, please. That was, obviously, the wrong answer."

Once again, Rob did as he was told.

"Right, question three. You're going to get this one, Rob. I can feel it in my bones. Arthur Wellesley was better known as the duke of where?"

"Oh, that's an easy one," Rob said with a smile. "Hazard."

"Come again," Jammin said.

"The answer is Hazard," Rob repeated, sure as sure could be he'd nailed the question.

"The duke of Hazard? You know that's the wrong answer, right?"

Rob didn't answer. He took a step forward, looking utterly deflated.

"Two more wrong answers and you're in the sea, my friend. Okay next question, and I want you to really think about this one. Name a film starring Bob Hoskins that's also the name of a painting by Leonardo da Vinci?"

Once again, Rob gave the impression of a man mulling over an answer, and once again, he didn't have a clue.

"I'm gonna have to push you for an answer," Jammin insisted.

"I've got it," Rob said, snapping his fingers triumphantly. "Who Framed Roger Rabbit?"

"Oh, for fuck's sake." Jammin removed his sunglasses and rubbed his eyes in frustration. "You think that Da Vinci painted Roger Rabbit?"

"He could've done," Rob snapped. "He was a cartoon Rabbit. Someone had to draw him."

"Just ask the next fucking question," Rob barked, taking a step forward without having to be asked.

"Fine," Jammin said, shaking his head. "Either real or fictional, name a famous Willy?"

"Oh, fuck me, that's easy. Willy the Pooh."

"Well, that's incredible," Jammin said. "You haven't managed to get a single question right. Might as well not delay the inevitable." He nodded towards the end of the plank. "In you go, my friend."

Rob, accepting his fate, stepped off the end of the plank, turning to give the laughing crowd the bird as he tumbled into the crystal blue water below.

"Next to walk the plank, Alice Hunt. Step on up, Alice. And for the love of God, try to do better than the last guy."

Ollie watched as Chris approached with two of the most flamboyant drinks he'd ever seen. The liquid inside the glasses was bright blue, and all manner of

26

decorative trash, from little umbrellas to sticks with cherries and olives and who knew what else, made it look almost impossible to drink.

"Did you see that guy walk the plank?" Ollie asked, taking a drink from Chris and holding it up to examine it.

"Forget about that shit," Chris replied. "You need to come and see this bartender. He's doing all that shit that dude does in that movie."

"What shit? What dude? What movie?"

"You know? That movie where they throw the bottles over their heads. It's got that weird little fucker in it."

"What are you talking about?" Ollie asked, frustrated.

"The weird little actor guy. The one with the big teeth who believes in aliens and shit."

"You mean Tom Cruise?"

That's the one," Chris said, patting his friend on the shoulder. He's doing all that shit that Tom Cruise does in the movie, where he makes cocktails. I can't remember what it's called."

"Cocktail," Ollie reminded him.

"Is it?"

"Yeah, dumbass. The film is called Cocktail."

"So, why was I thinking Top Gun?" Chris asked.

"That's a film about fighter plans. Jesus Christ, Ollie, watch a movie from time to time."

Alice Hunt had fared better than Rob before her. She'd answered two questions correctly. Unfortunately this wasn't enough to save her, and she eventually ended up in the sea next to Rob.

"Two down," Jammin called to the crowd. Who's next, and will they survive to see the next round?"

The next three rounds saw mixed results. Two guys stepped up to the plank, and both ended up in the water. The only winner so far had been a small blonde girl named Laurie who looked a bit like Bond villain, Jaws' girlfriend in Moonraker with her pigtails and big, round glasses.

Sarah ran over to have her go, having just heard her name called by the resident DJ. She jumped around in jubilation, her exposed breasts bouncing around shamelessly.

'That bitch doesn't give a single fuck,' Maggie thought, watching her friend. She had to admit she was deeply envious. She would have loved to be as carefree as Sarah, but sadly she wasn't wired that way. Maggie had made peace with the fact that she had too many hang-ups. Still, she'd come away to this retreat, and even though she did her best to cover herself as much as possible, she still stood on the deck of a ship, butt naked in front of strangers. That, she knew to be true, was progress.

Amazingly, Sarah had gotten her first few questions right. That was to be as close to victory as she would come, as every question after that received an incorrect answer. Eventually, she found herself at the end of the line.

"I had high hopes for you, Sarah," Jammin said, not even trying to hide the fact that he was checking out her butt. "Are you ready for your next question?"

"Yes," Sarah snapped.

"Someone doesn't like to lose," Jammin smirked. "Okay, to keep you high and dry, where are Bugatti cars made?"

"Ooh, I know this," Sarah chirped. "Italy. The answer is Italy."

"I'm sorry," Jammin said, shaking his head. "The answer is France."

"No, it's not. The answer is fucking Italy."

"Nope, afraid not. The founder is Italian, but the car is actually made in France. Sorry."

Sarah clenched her fists and gritted her teeth, enraged.

"You know what you have to do," Jammin said, pointing at the sea.

"Fuck this game," Sarah growled. She lifted her leg and began to step off when she spotted a large shape in the water. Sarah tried to stop her momentum, but it was too late to save herself. She was past the point of no return and committed to the jump. As she toppled over the side, she screamed. One word. "Shark!"

"What did she just say?" Chris asked.
"It sounded like Shark," Ollie replied. "Probably her idea of a joke."

Sarah barely hit the water before being snatched by the giant fish. It sprang from the depths like a torpedo and hit Sarah like a freight train, clamping its jaws shut and driving its razor-sharp teeth into her torso.
Sarah tried to scream again, but the blood that surged into her throat produced more of a drowning gurgle before spewing forth like a geyser and splattering her pain-twisted face. Taking another bite, the shark bit Sarah clean in half. Her guts spilt free from her mutilated abdomen and slid down the gullet of the beast.

Panic set in amongst the unlucky few who found themselves afloat in a sea of blood and gore. They pounded frantically on the ship's hull, screaming and pleading to be pulled aboard. The absence of a ladder meant they had no escape from the terror that swam amongst them, ravenous for more flesh.

Meanwhile, on deck, everyone surged forward to get a better look at what was taking place in the water below.

"Get the fuck out of the way," Rob yelled as he pushed his way through the panicked swimmers. With total disregard for the welfare of anyone but himself, he tried to climb onto the shoulders of Alice, who had been busy looking for a way to scale the side of the boat. His weight caught her off guard, pushing her beneath the surface and causing Rob to tumble back into the sea.

Rob turned to swim up for air when he felt an intense pressure on his leg, followed by instant sickening pain. Not daring to look back, he tried in vain to swim up. It took him a second to register that he was travelling backwards, away from the surface. His lungs screamed for air, and Rob's survival instinct kicked in. He kicked at the shark with his free foot and, to his amazement, after landing a couple of solid hits the fish let go. Rob, seizing the chance to get away, made a break for it and powered towards fresh air. Triumphantly, he broke the surface and desperately consumed large gulps of oxygen.

Rob's fingers tentatively worked their way down his thigh towards the area where the shark had bitten him. His heart pounded in his chest as he investigated the extent of his injuries, terrified that he would find his limb to be missing. To his relief, the leg was still intact, albeit with a couple of large wounds where the animal's serrated teeth had penetrated his flesh.

"Fuck, yeah," Rob cried out in relief, pounding his fist into the water. "Still got my fucking leg."

The Great White came barrelling past like a freight train and took Rob's leg clean off in one swift, precise bite.

Rob puked into the sea before blacking out.

Dessert

"We need to help them," Maggie said as she surveyed the carnage below. "Where's that fucking DJ?"

Jammin, unbeknownst to Maggie stood behind her, wide-eyed and pale-faced, as he watched the people in the water being torn to shreds.

"That shit isn't my job," he protested.

"Well, whose job is it?" Maggie snapped. "You're the one in charge of this fucking party. And, for the love of god, please stop pressing your ridiculous cock against me before I cut it off and feed it to the fish."

"This hardly seems like a good time for a drink," Ollie said as his friend headed back to the bar.

"I'm not getting a drink, dickhead," Chris shouted back. "I'm being proactive."

"What?"

"I'm saving the fucking day."

Chris leaned over the bar and grabbed a bottle of vodka. Twisting the cap free, he took a cloth and splashed it with the alcohol before shoving the wet rag into the top of the bottle. He took a box of complimentary matches from a basket on the end of the bar and used them to light the booze-soaked cloth before turning and marching heroically back towards the side of the boat.

"What are you doing?" Ollie asked, alarmed by the makeshift Molotov Cocktail that his friend held above his head.

"I'm gonna torch that motherfucking shark," Chris grunted.

"Shouldn't we do something to help?" Anita asked, throwing her arms up in despair and knocking the flaming bottle of vodka out of Chris' hand.

The bottle tumbled from his grip, spilling its contents over Anita. The flaming rag ignited the alcohol, instantly engulfing the unfortunate blonde in flames.

Anita took off running. Her skin burning away, layer by ruined layer. Her piercing screams alerting the remaining party guests to her tormented plight.

During the party, such a vast quantity of alcohol had been spilt that as Anita ran around in a state of anguished panic, the flames that danced around her blistering flesh ignited the deck, spreading with such speed that it quickly became an insurmountable inferno.

Anita, overcome by her injuries, tumbled to the floor, a blackened husk.

Those who remained on deck found themselves backed against the railings by the intense heat of the fire that now consumed the ship. The hellish blaze devoured everything in its path, leaving no potential escape route other than over the side of the ship.

"We need to jump," Jammin said, grabbing Riley by the arm.

"I'm not going in there with that thing," she snapped, yanking her arm free of his grip.

"You either jump and take your chances in the water or stay here and burn to death. Your choice."

Riley cried.

"I don't have time for this shit. Pull yourself together."

"I'm not a very good swimmer," Riley wept.

"Well, now's the time to learn," Jammin responded, grabbing her arm once again.

Jammin scooped up Riley and threw her over the side before she could protest. She cursed him all the way down. Unfortunately, Jammin hadn't bothered to check that the coast was clear before hurling her into the sea, and she landed hard on Alice Hunt's head, breaking the girl's neck and killing her instantly.

Alice floated lifeless for a second before being dragged beneath the waves by the blood-thirsty fish.

DJ Jammin plunged into the ocean, avoiding inflicting harm on anyone else. He surfaced, wiped the salt water from his eyes and began searching for Riley, who was nowhere to be seen.

Countless more bodies plummeted into the water to escape the fire above.

Ollie emerged first, followed closely by Chris, who coughed and spluttered to clear his lungs of the seawater he'd accidentally inhaled on impact.

"You okay?" Ollie asked, patting his friend on the back.

"No, I just swallowed half of the ocean."

"Well, this is another nice mess you've gotten me into," Ollie snapped.

"I'm sorry, Ollie," Chris replied.

Having swam around in circles, desperately searching for his companion, Jammin felt a swell of relief when he spotted Riley a few feet from where she'd originally entered the sea.

"Hey, Riley," Jammin called out as he swam towards her. There was no answer.

"Hey," he tried again. She still didn't answer. Jammin reached out and placed a hand on Riley's shoulder and gently shook her to get her attention.

"You okay, honey?"

Riley's mutilated corpse rolled over to expose the horror of her injuries. The left side of her torso had been sheared off by the monster shark. Everything from the arm, shoulder and even her left breast had been removed in the attack. The beast's teeth had also caught the girl's face, tearing a gaping hole in her left cheek, and exposing her jawbone.

Jammin opened his mouth and screamed. A scream that shouldn't have been possible for a man to produce unless that man is Jesse Walsh in Freddy's Revenge.

Maggie had been the last person to leap from the burning ship. Not being able to swim, she found herself between a rock and a hard place, or in this case, a wet and a hot place. She breached the water and immediately sank, thrashing her arms and legs in a desperate panic.

Luckily, Ollie had spotted her and dove to retrieve her. Grabbing her flailing hand, Ollie pulled her close and then dragged her up for air. Pumped with adrenaline, Ollie was yet to notice that his glasses were on their way to the ocean floor.

Maggie coughed violently, desperate to expel the water from her lungs.

"You okay?" Ollie asked, pushing her wet hair from her face.

"Yeah, thank you," Maggie struggled to say between gasps.

"What the fuck just happened?" Chris asked, swimming over.

"I don't swim well," Maggie replied.

"You don't swim? Well, what the fuck are you doing on a boat?"

"I wasn't planning on ending up in the sea," Maggie barked. "I can swim, just not well."

"You could have at least grabbed a life jacket."

"Don't you think I hadn't thought of that?" she snapped. "All the life jackets are on fire, you fucking dimwit."

Everyone who'd been aboard the party boat was now in the water. The initial shouts of panic had given way to an eerie quiet. Those who hadn't yet been mauled by the killer fish now bobbed helplessly in the gentle waves, too afraid to make any noise and draw attention to themselves.

The sea itself resembled a butcher's sink. Bits of mangled remains and human blood and guts made for a disgusting, macabre stew. Those still living were the dumplings.

DJ Jammin floated aimlessly on his back in a state of shock. His once Perma-erect, ridiculously oversized penis had given up the ghost and now flopped lifelessly on his abdomen.

"Look at that thing," Maggie said, unable to take her eyes off of Jammin's wilted phallus. "Why does anyone need a dick that big? It's unnatural."

"I think we have bigger things to worry about than a cheesy parody of a party host's dick," Chris replied.

"Where's the shark?" Ollie asked.

"Good question," Maggie responded. It hasn't attacked anyone for a while now."

"Maybe it's full," Chris joked. "Eyes were bigger than its belly."

"Funny," Maggie replied, rolling her eyes.

For the first time in his life, Jammin didn't know how to handle a situation. He'd often been quick with a quip to defuse an escalating problem. Failing that, he would rely on his intimidating stature to back down an aggressor. This time, however, he found himself in a predicament he couldn't talk or bully his way out of. His girls were dead, his party boat was sinking, and he found himself cast adrift and at the mercy of a ravenous sea monster. All hope had abandoned Jammin, so he just lay there, letting the current take him.

'Jammin,' he thought. *'Why did I choose such a shit name?'* He smiled to himself, feeling suddenly silly and

embarrassed. His real name, Hector Dennis, wouldn't have had the same ring to it as DJ Jammin. He'd chosen Jammin because whenever anyone had asked him how easily he found having sex with such an enormous cock, he'd always answered that he would just 'jam it in.' Only now, having nothing to do but reflect on stupid little details, did he realise how shit his chosen moniker was.

'Jammin,' he thought again, laughing to himself. *'What a cunt.'*

Something large gently bumped Jammin from beneath the surf, snapping him away from his thoughts. He felt his chest tighten with anxiety, robbing him of his breath. Not because the thing which had bumped him had done so with enough force to knock the wind from within him, but because he knew what the thing was.

"Oh, fuck, oh fuck, oh fuck," Jammin muttered, frantically searching for a sign of the killer fish.

His eyes nervously searched the water until they spotted it. A huge, dark shape cruising towards him. Jammin turned and swam. He pumped his arms with every ounce of strength he could call upon, desperate to escape the approaching death. That's when he spotted her.

The heavy-set girl Jammin had cruelly mocked earlier in the day did her best to tread water. Her cheeks flushed red with exertion caused by the prolonged workout required, just to keep her head above the waves. She didn't notice the obnoxious DJ heading in her direction.

'You'll do,' Jammin thought as he swam up to the fat girl with the red, sweaty face. The shark was almost upon him. It opened its jaws wide, ready to sink its teeth into the party host with the stupid name. Jammin wasted no time. He grabbed the girl and positioned her between him and the beast as it bore down on him, ready to deliver a killer bite. Jammin pushed the girl into the open maw of the animal.

The shark, not expecting such a meal, thrashed as the girl's plump frame filled its mouth, trying to either bite through her or shake her loose, but the girl had become wedged. She began screaming, the horror of her situation being too much to comprehend.

"Fuck, yeah," Jammin yelled triumphantly. "That'll keep it busy for a while."

Still struggling, desperate to free itself of the large meaty gobstopper, the shark dove beneath the surface, taking the unfortunate, big girl with it.

Cheese and Coffee

An hour had passed since they'd last spotted the razor-toothed menace. The ship had finally succumbed to the fire and was now on its way to the ocean floor. There had been no signs of rescue. The best they could hope for was that the shark choked to death on the more than ample meal the large girl had provided.

"How much longer do you think we'll be out here?" Maggie asked.

"If nobody's looking for us, it might be days, maybe weeks," Chris replied.

"It won't be that long," Ollie interrupted, trying to add a positive spin to their situation. "We are, most likely, in a fairly busy shipping lane. I'm sure someone will be by sometime soon."

"Doubt it," Chris grunted.

"Okay, captain pessimism. Well, based on your logic, we won't be out here for days or weeks because we will have died by then. Likely it'll be exposure, dehydration or a fucking enormous, prehistoric fish that'll kill us."

Maggie, no longer able to control her emotions, burst into tears.

"Look what you're doing," Chris said, looking pissed at his friend for scaring the girl. He slid his arm around Maggie to comfort her.

"Me?" Ollie said, looking wounded. "How the hell am I the bad guy?"

"Shh," Chris said with his finger to his lips. "You're making it worse."

"Un-fucking-believable," Ollie said, giving up.

"Erm, can you get your cock off my leg, please?" Maggie protested, wiping the tears from her eyes.

"Jesus, sorry," Chris replied, twisting his body to stop his penis from resting against her skin.

"Pervert," she snapped, shrugging off his arm.

"I wasn't trying it on," Chris protested.

"Classy," Ollie laughed. "Very classy."

"I said, stopping rubbing your fucking dick on my leg!" Maggie hollered.

"I'm fucking not," Chris said. "I swear."

"Well, something's rubbing against my leg."

Maggie barely finished her sentence before being tugged violently beneath the water. It all happened so fast that everyone who witnessed her vanishing under the waves did so in stunned silence, mouths agape.

"What the fuck?" Chris finally uttered. "Where'd she go?"

Ollie was just about to answer when Maggie blasted up from the depths, wailing.

"Oh shit," Ollie cried, reaching for her extended hand. He almost had her when her body jerked away from his grasp, dragged through the water at great speed, a slick of her blood streaking the water behind her.

"Fucking help me," she cried out. "It hurts. It hurts so bad."

Chris and Ollie gave chase, not giving much thought to what they would do if they caught up with her. Still, they swam as fast as they could, following the shrieking girl as she fought back against the creature that had her in its vice-like jaws. She punched and scratched and hammered on the animal's nose but still, it refused to let go.

"Go for its eyes," Ollie called out to her.

She must have heard him because that's exactly what Maggie did. She leaned over and rammed her long, pointed fingernail directly into the beast's right eye. The shark let go of her in an instant and vanished below to protect its badly damaged eye.

Ollie was the first to catch up with Maggie. He took her in his arms, allowing her to rest her head on his shoulder.

"You okay?" He asked.

"My leg hurts," she replied.

"Okay," Ollie said. "I'm gonna need to take a look at it."

Chris reached the pair, a look of concern on his sunburnt face.

"Here, take her," Ollie said, passing Maggie over to him.

"What are you doing?" Chris asked, taking the injured girl in his arms.

"I'm going to go check out her injuries."

"Oh, okay. Be careful."

Ollie took a deep breath and disappeared.

"I bet he's down there, trying to get a better look at my cooch," Maggie joked.

"Ollie isn't like that," Chris said in defence of his friend's honour.

'Wow,' Ollie thought. *'That is a nice cooch.'*

He reprimanded himself for getting side-tracked and turned his attention to her leg, squinting to better focus now that his glasses lived at the bottom of the ocean.

Thankfully, the damage was minimal. The shark's teeth had missed the major artery, and the wounds were shallow. The greatest danger came from the blood that seeped from the gashes into the surrounding water.

Ollie, happy with his non-professional diagnosis, was just about to make his ascent and deliver the good news when he spotted it. The man-eater was back. It emerged from the gloomy depths and made a beeline for a pair of legs that dangled aimlessly a few feet away.

Between the clueless swimmer's legs hung the biggest dick that Ollie had ever seen, and he needed no guesses as to who it belonged to. Ollie thrust himself skyward to alert the blissfully ignorant idiot DJ.

Jammin saw the beast coming straight for him. In a desperate attempt to escape the monster's jaws, he thrust himself sideways just as the shark bore down on him. He would have avoided the animal altogether had it not been for his oversized pecker, which hadn't quite cleared the shark's path. As the creature's jaws snapped shut, one of its jagged teeth pierced his member and became wedged in the thick meat of his penis. Jammin squealed, his pride and joy skewered on the dagger-like tooth.

"It's got me!" Jammin screamed as the shark dragged him along by the shlong. "It's got me by the cock!"

The survivors watched in horror as the DJ was towed away by the dick, shrieking like a young boy who'd accidentally caught his wang in his zipper.

As he pounded his fists on the shark's head, the animal shook him. Violently, Jammin fought back, kicking and punching, and was suddenly free.

"Yes!" He shouted victoriously. "I fucking beat you." He thrust his fist into the air in triumph, and that's when the pain hit him.

Jammin doubled over as the hurt tore through his abdomen. He felt around for the cause of his anguish only to discover what he knew to be true but feared to confirm. Where once existed a magnificent example of the male member, now remained a shredded, mangled mess of tissue and torn dick skin. The thrashing of the shark had caused its saw-like tooth to carve deeper through Jammin's chopper, weakening it enough that one brutal shake later, the mutilated penis was ripped from the DJ's groin.

Jammin blacked out, the shock of losing his pride and joy proving too much.

"Well, that should keep him fed for a while," Chris remarked, watching the shark swim away with the DJ's tackle between its teeth.

"How's that funny?" Ollie responded, punching his friend on the arm. "He's most likely going to die from his injury. If he isn't eaten first."

"Being eaten would be a mercy killing at this point," Maggie said.

"We should do something," Ollie said. "Help him out, maybe."

Chris shook his head.

"We can't just leave him there like this," Ollie snapped.

"What do you want us to do? Chase down the shark, steal the guy's dick back and glue it back on?"

"Don't be ridiculous."

"He's right," Maggie interrupted.

"Thanks," Ollie replied.

"I didn't mean you," Maggie said. "I mean him." She motioned towards Chris with a nod. "If we help him, we'll be swimming around in even more blood. That thing out there won't have gone far, and we'll be putting ourselves on the menu."

"We're already on the menu," Ollie replied. "Hey, where is he?"

They'd been so busy bickering they hadn't noticed the fish return and pull the wounded DJ down into a watery grave.

Sheer panic swept over Chris as he scanned the sea for a sign that Jammin was still with him. It was only while looking for the castrated party host that it finally dawned on him just how hopeless their situation was. Not only could he not see the DJ, but everyone else who'd fled the burning ship had vanished, too. Taken by the shark without them seeing.

An icy chill crept over him, and Chris suddenly found it hard to breathe.

"You okay?" Ollie asked. "You're as white as a sheet."

"They've all gone."

"What's he talking about?" Maggie asked.

"They've all gone," Chris repeated. "We're all that's left."

He was right. They were the only survivors. Their chances of being attacked had whittled down to one in three as they bobbed hopelessly in a soup of human offal, the only remnants of the other revellers.

"We're going to die out here," Chris added.

"We need to swim for it," Maggie said.

"You're kidding," Ollie responded in disbelief. "We are miles from shore, and you've got an injured leg. We won't be getting far."

"Okay, and what's the alternative?" Maggie asked. "Are we just going to float around until it's our time to be eaten? I don't see that we've got a choice."

"She's right," Chris said. "We stay here, and we're dead for sure. I say we swim."

"We won't make it," Ollie protested.

"Then we don't make it," Maggie replied. "But anything has to be better than waiting here to die. I'd rather die trying than give up and let the fucker kill me."

"Fine," Ollie said, defeated.

"Let's go before it comes back," Chris said, already pulling away at a swift pace.

A Wafer-Thin Mint

They'd been swimming for twenty minutes before Maggie's leg forced them to take a break. There had been no sign of the shark, and Ollie commented, on a few occasions, how it was probably busy devouring one of its many victims back at the site where the boat had gone down.

Ollie's optimistic attitude was met with a double-barrelled dose of negativity, as both Maggie and Chris pointed out that they couldn't be certain it wasn't following behind, waiting for the right opportunity to strike and take one of them out.

Being ambushed by the aquatic predator wasn't their only concern. They hadn't caught so much as a whiff of land yet, and as Maggie had so insistently informed them, they could easily be swimming further out to sea.

Just as it seemed that all hope was lost, an object in the distance caught Chris' eye.

"You see that?" he asked.

"What?" they both replied in unison.

"Look, over there," Chris pointed.

"I don't see anything," Maggie said, shielding her eyes from the glare of the sun.

"Oh, wait," Ollie chimed in. "I see it. Is that a boat?"

"I think it is, buddy," Chris replied, elated. "Come on, let's go."

It took them much longer than they'd expected to reach the object that had indeed turned out to be a boat.

Maggie's bad leg and lack of swimming ability had slowed them down, but thankfully the shark was still noticeable in its absence. Chris was the first one to make it to what turned out to be a small speedboat. He pulled himself up out of the water and into the vessel, relieved to be out of the sea. His body hurt from all the swimming, and he lay for a few seconds, completely exhausted.

Ollie climbed into the boat, followed swiftly by Maggie, who he helped to clamber in.

"Thank god," Ollie spluttered. His chest heaving, exhausted from the lengthy swim. "I've never been so happy to not be in the water."

Maggie, however, wasn't so joyful. She could now get a good look at the extent of the damage to her leg, and while Ollie was right, and it wasn't as bad as she had first feared, the bite marks looked as though an infection had set in. The skin around the puncture wounds had turned red and now itched, which she figured couldn't be good.

"How's the leg?" Ollie asked.

"It's seen better days," Maggie replied.

"Let me look."

The lacerations appeared to be in the early stages of infection, but Ollie wasn't too concerned yet.

"You'll live," he said, trying to reassure her. "Once we get this boat back to dry land, we can get you to a hospital. A few antibiotics, and you'll be as good as new."

A disturbance in the water beside them caused the three of them to sit up straight, their hearts in their mouths.

"What was that?" Maggie whispered.

"I don't know," Chris replied.

A dark figure exploded from beneath the waves. They all jumped as the figure landed on the side of the boat with a thud.

"Jesus fucking Christ," Chris hollered. "It's just a diver."

The diver threw his spear gun into the boat and removed his regulator from his mouth. A fish wriggled around, desperately clinging to what little life it had left as it bled out on the deck.

"What the fuck are you lot doing on my boat?" the diver asked.

The three of them just stared at the new arrival, too shocked to form words.

"I was down there for forty minutes, and when I come back, there's an idiot convention on my boat. You three had better come up with some answers. Who the fuck are you, and why the fuck are you all butt-naked? This better not be some kinda orgy or something."

"I'm sorry, mister," Ollie blurted out. "Our boat sank, and a shark attacked us. Everyone else is dead."

"Boy, that sounds like some prime rib bullshit. There aint any man-eating sharks in these waters. Hasn't been for years."

"He's telling the truth," Chris piped in.

"So, what happened to your britches then? Shark eat your clothes?"

"No, sir," Ollie said. "We were at a naturist party."

"Oh, you're from that pervert island, aint you?"

The diver pulled his mask off, and threw it in the boat where it landed next to his spear gun.

"We really need your help, sir," Ollie pleaded. "Our friend is injured."

"What happened to her?" the diver asked, oblivious to the injuries on Maggie's leg as he was now too busy gawking at her breasts.

Maggie noticed and covered them with her arm.

"The shark did that," Ollie replied. It attacked her, but she got away.

The diver paused for a moment as if weighing up his options.

"Help us, please," Maggie pleaded.

The diver flashed her a grin that exposed his brown, broken teeth.

"Please," she repeated.

"Okay, okay. I'll help you."

"Thanks, mister," Ollie said gratefully.

"Just give me a hand, will ya?" He reached towards Ollie, wanting to be pulled into the boat. Ollie took his hand to assist.

The Great White slammed into the side of the boat like a torpedo, crushing the diver between its jaws and tipping the others back into the sea. It bit down on the hapless, squealing man, breaking his spine as its nightmarish teeth punctured his torso, rupturing multiple organs in the process. The diver opened his mouth to scream but was silenced by the torrent of blood that spewed forth and sprayed the hull of the capsized speedboat.

The fish continued to bite into its victim, each chomp slicing deeper into the unfortunate man's flesh. Still the diver didn't die. He suffered through every chew, even when his broken body separated at the midriff and his lower half slid down the gullet of the hungry beast. His top half quickly followed, the diver still conscious and alert as he slowly disappeared down the shark's throat.

Cheque, Please

"It ate the fucking diver!" Ollie yelled. "It fucking ate him alive."

"Calm down," Maggie shouted, trying to make herself heard over the panic.

"It fucking ate him, and we're next!"

Maggie's palm connected hard with Ollie's cheek, shocking him into silence.

"Calm the fuck down," she repeated.

Chris watched the shark dive beneath the overturned boat.

"The shark's coming straight for us," Ollie said, his voice trembling.

"Let it come," Chris replied, balling his hand into a fist. "Come get me, you ugly fucker."

The fish streaked towards Chris as he drew his fist back, ready to strike the predator. The enormous animal approached at an alarming speed, but Chris wasn't about to go out without a fight.

Suddenly, the shark changed course, zipping past Chris and heading for Ollie.

"Ollie, move! Get out of the way!" Chris called out, but it was too late.

Ollie couldn't react in time to save himself, and before he'd realised what was happening, he felt pain. Instant, agonising pain.

Maggie drifted over to Chris and buried her head into his chest to avoid having to witness the horrific mauling that Ollie was being subjected to.

Chris didn't look away. He watched as the fish tore his friend apart, swallowing Ollie a piece at a time. He saw the entire spectacle, and rage boiled up in his veins.

"I'm gonna kill that motherfucker," Chris said, pushing Maggie away.

"What? How?"

"Get to the boat and climb up on top. I'm ending this shit right now."

"But…"

"Get on the boat, now!" Chris yelled.

Maggie obeyed. She swam over to the capsized boat and dragged herself up to the relative safety it provided.

"Okay, fucknut," Chris grunted through gritted teeth. "Time to make a shit-tonne of sushi."

The shark circled Chris as he dove to retrieve the divers' speargun. The oxygen tank that the man had used had been damaged in the attack, so Chris had to hope he could hold his breath long enough to make it back to the surface.

As luck would have it, he didn't need to waste any time searching for the weapon. Visibility was on his side, and the gun was easy to locate. Chris seized the speargun and headed back for air.

The shark made its first attack run as Chris made his ascent. It roared towards him, mouth agape and ready to make the kill, but Chris had anticipated the ambush. As the beast charged him, he was able to roll clear of the monster's deadly jaws and counterattack. As the fish missed its mark, Chris plunged the spear into its eye. The animal thrashed its head wildly, and Chris pulled the spear from its destroyed eyes socket and made haste for the surface.

Erupting from the surf, Chris gasped to fill his lungs with oxygen. He'd pushed his ability to hold his breath to breaking point, fearing he would black out before reaching the top.

As air flooded his screaming chest, he swore he could hear the faint sound of a woman's voice.

"It's coming right for you," Maggie called out, trying to get his attention.

Chris wiped the saltwater from his eyes and spotted Maggie waving hysterically at him.

"What?" He yelled back.

"Shark," she screamed. "Behind you!"

Chris turned to see the large fin rushing towards him.

"Shit."

The shark made a grab for his leg but somehow missed by mere inches. Chris, not believing his luck, took hold of the rampaging creature's dorsal fin and found himself dragged along with such brutality that it almost tore his arm from the socket. As he pulled himself on top of the fish, it bucked from side to side in an effort to eject the unwanted passenger.

Knowing that the shark could head below the waves at any second, Chris needed to act fast. He placed the tip of the spear gun against the shark's head, hoping and praying that he had located its brain. He didn't have time to second guess himself. His aim would have to do.

"Smile, you son of a cunt!" He shouted, pulling the trigger and firing the spear deep into the Great White's cranium.

The shark stopped thrashing. Its speed slowed, and it sank into the ocean. Chris bailed off and watched as the beast disappeared beneath the water.

Back on the upturned boat, Maggie whooped and hollered in celebration.

Chris watched as she bounced around joyously and smiled to himself. He figured if he could get them back to shore and get her leg treated, he might be in with a shot, given all they'd been through together.

'Maybe it won't be a completely wasted vacation after all,' he thought.

"We need to turn this boat back over," Chris said as Maggie slid back down into the sea.

Maggie didn't respond. Instead, she moved herself up close to Chris and pressed her naked body against his. Her arms snaked around him, and she pulled him closer, crushing her breasts against his chest.

"But, your leg," Chris said, his voice a nervous quiver.

"What're a few more minutes going to hurt?" she asked.

Before Chris could reply, she pressed her lips against his, kissing him passionately.

Chris pulled away gently and smiled.

"You sure you want to do this now?"

"Of course," she said with a smile. "You saved us. You're a hero, and heroes are fucking hot."

She kissed him again, harder, and her hands ran down to his butt. This time, he didn't resist.

The shark surged up from the depths like a surface-to-air missile. It breached the waves with such speed that its entire body left the water. With one powerful bite, it decapitated the kissing couple and disappeared beneath the waves, taking their disembodied heads with it.

About The Author

Lee Richmond was born in the swampy marshlands of East Anglia. Fed on a steady diet of fast, snotty punk rock and 80s slasher movies, it was only a matter of time before the sick, twisted imagery that festered in his head eventually found its way to the page. Lee was influenced from a very early age by the films of John Carpenter, Dario Argento, Wes Craven and Tobe Hooper and the books of Clive Barker, Stephen King, and James Herbert. Music also plays its part in influencing Lee's writing. His love for bands like The Misfits, Ramones, Fugazi and Sisters of Mercy and the works of such movie composers as Hans Zimmer and Christopher *Lee's other interests include playing bass guitar and drawing. He also owns and writes for horror movie website, reelhorrorshow.co.uk along with fellow writer, Mark Green.

Coming Soon...

Gary is a ghost tasked with haunting an apartment in Greenwich Village, New York. It's a pretty easy gig for the lazy spectre, until the Freeborne's move in. Gary half-heartedly sets about trying to frighten the family into fleeing their new residence. What should have been a simple haunting takes a dark turn when Gary comes up against the Freeborne's young daughter, Pandora. The little girl is not all she seems, and Gary begins to realise that he may not be the scariest thing in the building.

More From ReelHorrorShow Publications

232 Jericho Avenue – Lee Richmond

Beneath – Lee Richmond

FROM THE AUTHOR OF 232 JERICHO AVENUE

BENEATH

LEE RICHMOND

Jingle Hells — Lee Richmond & Mark MJ Green

Medley Of The Macabre – Lee Richmond & Mark MJ Green

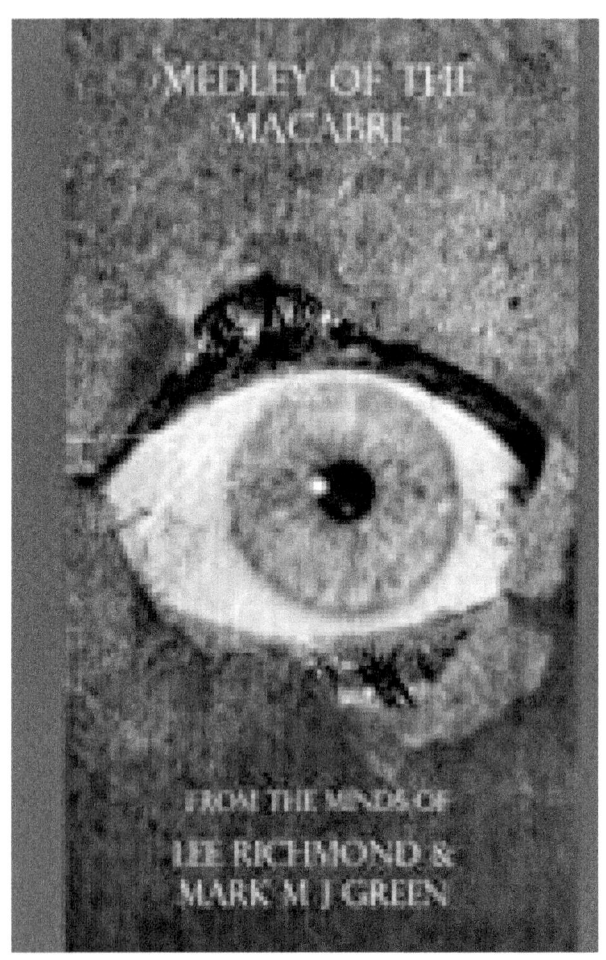

Contact ReelHorrorShow Publications:

reelhorrorshow@hotmail.com

or

Head on over to the ReelHorrorShow
Podcast available on Spotify.

Printed in Great Britain
by Amazon

47102125R00040